Flash
and the
Butterfly

by Jill Atkins and Sue Eastland

W

Flash and Flick lived in a big field.

They had lots of grass to eat.

They could run around and play.

One day, Flash trotted over to Flick.

"Come and play," he said.

"Don't go too far," said his mum.

"You might get lost."

"We will be careful," said Flash,

and he galloped away across the field.

"Wait for me!" called Flick.

She chased after him.

Flick and Flash stopped to eat
some fresh, green grass.

A butterfly flew by.

It fluttered from flower to flower.

"Oh, look! Isn't it beautiful," said Flick.

Just then, the butterfly flew away.

"Let's follow it," said Flash.

"But we might get lost," said Flick,

looking back at her mother.

But Flash went on running.

Away he went, after the butterfly.

Flash came to a hedge.

He had to stop, but the butterfly didn't.

"Wait for me!" Flash said to the butterfly.

But the butterfly flew on over the hedge,

into a lane.

Flash pushed through the hedge.

The butterfly flew along the lane.

Flash trotted along behind it.

The butterfly flew into the wood
and Flash followed.

He watched the butterfly

fly in and out of the trees.

But suddenly it disappeared!

"Where are you, butterfly?" he called.

Flash looked all around but
he couldn't see the butterfly.
And he didn't know where he was.
The trees all looked the same!

"I think I'll go this way," he said.

Then he stopped and looked behind him.

"No, I'll go that way," he said.

He stopped again.

Oh no! Flash was lost!

Flash trotted for a long time.

It started to get dark.

He saw two bright eyes in the darkness.

He heard a hoot in the trees.

Flash was scared.

"I want to go home," said Flash,

starting to cry.

He curled up on some soft moss

and cried himself to sleep.

"What is a horse doing out here

in the wood?" said a voice.

Flash woke up with a jump.

A rabbit was looking at him.

"I was chasing a butterfly and I got lost,"

said Flash. "Can you help me get home

to my mum?"

But the rabbit shook his head.

"I'd like to help you, but I don't know where your mum is," he said.

A squirrel came down from a tree to talk to Flash.

"Can you help me get home?" said Flash.

The squirrel shook her head.

"I can't help you. I don't know where you live," she said. "Maybe the owl knows."

The owl flew down to talk to Flash.

"I ran a long way away from my field,"

said Flash. "And now I am lost.

Can you help me find my way back home?"

"I will go and fly across the fields,"

said the owl. "I may be able to see

your mum."

Soon, the owl came back.

"There are horses in the big field," he called.

"I can take you there. Follow me."

They came to the hedge and Flash
pushed his way through.

"Thank you," he said to the rabbit,
the squirrel and the owl.

"Look, there's my mum!"

He galloped across the field.

Mum was glad to see Flash
but she was cross, too.

"Where have you been?" she asked.

"I'm sorry, Mum," said Flash. "I followed
a butterfly. It disappeared and I got lost."

"Don't ever do something so silly again,"
said Mum.

"No, Mum," replied Flash. "I won't."

He trotted over to play with Flick.

"Were you scared?" she asked.

"Yes, I was a bit," said Flash.

"I didn't find the butterfly,

but I did find some new friends."

Story order

Look at these 5 pictures and captions.
Put the pictures in the right order
to retell the story.

1

The owl showed Flash the way.

2

Flash followed the butterfly.

3

Flash got lost in the wood.

4

Flash found his mum.

5

Flash and Flick saw a butterfly.

Independent Reading

This series is designed to provide an opportunity for your child to read on their own. These notes are written for you to help your child choose a book and to read it independently.

In school, your child's teacher will often be using reading books which have been banded to support the process of learning to read. Use the book band colour your child is reading in school to help you make a good choice. *Flash and the Butterfly* is a good choice for children reading at Purple Band in their classroom to read independently.

The aim of independent reading is to read this book with ease, so that your child enjoys the story and relates it to their own experiences.

About the book

Flash is a young foal who likes to explore. His mother warns him not to go too far away, but when he spots a beautiful butterfly, he has to follow it, no matter where he ends up!

Before reading

Help your child to learn how to make good choices by asking:
"Why did you choose this book? Why do you think you will enjoy it?"
Look at the cover together and ask: "What do you think the story will be about?" Ask your child to think of what they already know about the story context. Then ask your child to read the title aloud. Ask: "Who do you think Flash is in the story?" Remind your child that they can sound out the letters to make a word if they get stuck.

Decide together whether your child will read the story independently or read it aloud to you.

During reading

Remind your child of what they know and what they can do independently. If reading aloud, support your child if they hesitate or ask for help by telling the word. If reading to themselves, remind your child that they can come and ask for your help if stuck.

After reading

Support comprehension by asking your child to tell you about the story. Use the story order puzzle to encourage your child to retell the story in the right sequence, in their own words. The correct sequence can be found on the next page.

Help your child think about the messages in the book that go beyond the story and ask: "Why doesn't Flick follow him? Why is Flash's mother cross with him at the end of the story?"

Give your child a chance to respond to the story: "How do you keep yourself safe? What would you do if you got lost? Who could you ask for help?"

Extending learning

Help your child think more about the inferences in the story by asking: "Do you think Flash will be more careful about wandering too far away in the future? Explain why he would or would not be."

In the classroom, your child's teacher may be teaching how to use speech marks when characters are speaking. There are many examples in this book that you could look at with your child. Find these together and point out how the end punctuation (comma, full stop, question mark or exclamation mark) comes inside the speech marks. Ask the child to read some examples out loud, adding appropriate expression.

Franklin Watts
First published in Great Britain in 2018
by The Watts Publishing Group

Copyright © The Watts Publishing Group 2018
All rights reserved.

Series Editors: Jackie Hamley and Melanie Palmer
Series Advisors: Dr Sue Bodman and Glen Franklin
Series Designer: Peter Scoulding

A CIP catalogue record for this book is
available from the British Library.

ISBN 978 1 4451 6223 2 (hbk)
ISBN 978 1 4451 6221 8 (pbk)
ISBN 978 1 4451 6222 5 (library ebook)

Printed in China

Franklin Watts
An imprint of
Hachette Children's Group
Part of The Watts Publishing Group
Carmelite House
50 Victoria Embankment
London EC4Y 0DZ

An Hachette UK Company
www.hachette.co.uk

www.franklinwatts.co.uk

FSC
www.fsc.org
MIX
Paper from
responsible sources
FSC® C104740

Answer to Story order: 5, 2, 3, 1, 4